Dark memories

J. Sharpe

www.jsharpefiction.com

First, a small gift

I want to thank you personally for downloading this book. You love to read, otherwise, you wouldn't have bought this book. So let me give you two exclusive free stories. Click here to watch the video.

In *In the arms of my love* the main character reincarnates into a flower and finds herself in some strange situations.

In *Treehouse* Grace is driving on the highway with two screaming eight-year-olds in the back seat and she's frustrated to say the least.

So when she sees a sign for a Rest Area, she's more than happy to pull over. The boys see the treehouse first. And when they climb its ladder, it's already too late. Then the screaming begins.

To get access to these stories and other free ones every month, simply click here or go to my website: www.jsharpefiction.com

You can help

Writing a novel is fun, but it also can be a hard and daunting task. Especially to make sure a lot of readers will find it and read it.

My dream is to be a full-time writer. I've traditional published 13 books so far in The Netherlands but still have a day job. Now the time is right to publish my books in other languages to, like this one, and chase my dreams furthermore.

And you can help me with that.

If you like this book, then please leave an honest review afterward. I love to read what you think.

For now: enjoy this rollercoaster.

J. Sharpe

Preface

*Note from the author.

This story will probably read as if it was completely made up. However, this is not (entirely) the case. Yours truly has experienced (almost) the same situation as the boy in this story. It contains more autobiographical elements than I can or will admit. That makes Dark memories one of the most precious, but also frightening stories I have written to date and also one that I don't like to read back myself.

That's said, I hope you will love it.

-1-

On my eighth birthday, I gave myself an imaginary friend.

My mother set the table. On the festive tablecloth, with green, yellow and red balls printed on it, lay dozens of plastic plates, candy and party hats. The room was decorated with balloons and there were chairs scattered across the room.

On the table was a quiche with eight candles in it. I actually wanted a cream pie, like the one I got for my birthday every year. But that was in England. In Portugal they didn't know what a cream pie was, apparently. I didn't even like quiche!

When it became clear that no one was coming, my mother's face turned grim. She hastily lit the candles, and I blew them out. I didn't eat a piece of the quiche. Instead, I opened the present my mother had wrapped herself. The package was rolled in toilet paper. It was a red truck, not much bigger than my finger. It lacked a mirror and the paint on the plastic roof was almost gone. It had eluded my mother that I had outgrown the car phase for over two years now.

I stood up. Because I didn't want to appear ungrateful, I put the truck in my pocket.

I wanted to walk to my room, but my mother stopped me. "Jerry?" Her trembling voice told me that she had started drinking early today. It sounded grating and slow.

I turned around. I didn't like to look my mother in the eye. It gave me the jitters. When she was sober she was a very kind woman, but unfortunately she hardly ever was anymore. She was usually either tipsy or totally wasted.

"I'm sorry nobody showed up," she said. "I invited everybody in your class, but ..." She stumbled over her words. She most definitely must have already finished a whole bottle of wine.

I glanced at the clock on the wall. It was only two o'clock in the afternoon. I tried to smile, but only half succeeded. I wanted to tell her that it didn't matter, that I knew that nobody would come. They were just kids I went to school with, not my friends. I didn't have any. Not anymore. Not here. But I remained silent.

With my head down, I walked outside.

We lived on the tip of a mountain. From the balcony that connected the two houses, the view of the village and the sea beyond was breathtaking.

Because the houses were relatively small, my father rented them both. The living room and kitchen were in the left building, we slept in the right one.

When I arrived in my room, I sat on my bed and sighed. The sharp plastic of the truck poked my leg. I pulled the toy out, looked at it again, and placed it on the shelf above my bed, where the only friend I did have looked at me cheerfully. Unfortunately, Tommy the teddy bear was never very talkative.

In England, I also didn't have many friends. I was a silent boy who preferred to be alone with a good book rather than play football outside. Still, there were one or two boys who, occasionally, hung out with me. But since the move, I had nobody at all.

That changed with the arrival of Mark.

-3-

Mark was invisible, except for me. I knew that from the moment I first saw him standing in one of the corners of my bedroom.

The open door squeaked shut. In the corner behind the door stood a boy with short, ruddy hair. He was covered in freckles.

He ran towards me with a grin from ear to ear. "Jerry, congratulations." He opened his arms and tried to hug me.

He went right through me.

I flew up. On my hands and knees, I crawled backwards over my bed until I reached the edge. I lost my balance and fell onto the carpet.

I gasped and looked up.

The boy bent over me, looked at his hands and sighed. As if ashamed, he ran his left hand through his hair and looked away. "Oh, that's right. I had completely forgotten about that. I can't touch you." Even though there was clearly a sadness and disappointment evident in his eyes, he conjured up a smile. "I'm Mark, but you already know that, don't you?"

"You're not real!" I said with a lump in my throat. "I'm dreaming this."

Mark looked at me as if he didn't quite understand. "You wanted a friend for your birthday, right?"

"A friend?"

Mark smiled. "Of course!"

There was a knock at the door. "Jerry, can I come in?"

Before I could answer, the door swung open. My father entered the room. He was a thin man. He had almost no hair on his head, but a big beard to compensate for that. If you looked at him, you wouldn't say he was a scuba diving instructor. Yet, no customer had ever complained. Quite the contrary. Everyone loved him for his warm and patient approach. When there were any costumers, that was.

When my father saw me lying on the floor, he rushed over to me. "What happened?"

I hurried to my feet. From the corner of my eye, I saw Mark looking mesmerized.

"Nothing," I answered quickly. "I fell out of bed, that's all."

Despite my explanation, my father glanced around the room. He looked directly at Mark. Twice! The boy just smiled at him, waved and even stuck his tongue out at him. My father didn't see it and I chuckled.

"What's so funny?" My father asked.

I shook my head. "Nothing."

My father looked at me. "Sometimes, I worry about you, Jerry."

I noticed that he was holding something behind his back. His cheeks turned red with shame when he gave me his present. "I'm sorry, kiddo. Next year we'll have money again for a real gift. I promise."

I recognized the book immediately. It had been in our bookcase in the living room for years. I had read it at least five times. "It doesn't matter, Dad," I said sincerely. Although I already knew how the story went, I was happy that the book now was mine and that I could put it on my own bookshelf. I had been dreaming for months of having my own library. There were only three books on the shelf above my bed at this moment, but you had to start somewhere, right?

My father gave me a pat on the head and left the room. It wasn't until the door closed behind him, that Mark dared to speak.

"He didn't even bother wrapping it for you."

I placed the book on the shelf. "He's a busy guy. Business isn't going to well. He only had three paying customers this month."

"Then how can he be busy?" Mark asked cynically.

I shrugged my shoulders. "My mother says we shouldn't have moved. That he selected the wrong location for his diving school."

"Typical for her to put the blame on him while she was the one who really wanted to live here," Mark replied with contempt in his voice. "Your father actually wanted to go to that place thirty miles away, don't you remember?"

"How do you know that?"

"I'm a figment of your imagination, Jerry. How can I not know that?"

-4-

That night my screaming parents woke me up, just like most nights before. The walls partially blocked the sound of their voices, but the screams were loud enough to get me out of a troubled dream.

Tired, I sat up in bed. I rubbed the sleep from my eyes and put my hand on my pounding head. When would they finally stop arguing?

The moon shone through a crack between the curtains and covered a part of my room in a white glow. The spooky image gave me the jitters. I hurriedly grabbed Tommy the teddy bear from the shelf and pressed him to my chest.

"It's always the same with you, Peter. You are a good-for-nothing, a fool." My mother clearly spoke with a double tongue.

"You shouldn't drink, Judith," my father shouted. "You know that. Why is it so difficult for you to leave the bottle alone?"

For a moment it was quiet, as if my mother was looking for a suitable answer. When she spoke, her words had extra power. It made my heart skip a beat.

'I HATE YOU!"

I swallowed and shivered. It wasn't the first time I heard my mother scream like that, but I couldn't get used to it, no matter how hard I tried.

I pulled the covers over my head. At times like this, I hated my parents. My mother because she was never satisfied with what she had, my father because he never really took action and kept believing her when she promised to stop drinking. However, they had sought help, back in England. Even my father had boundaries and a maximum to what he was willing to take from his wife. My mother endured two days of psychiatric help. On the third day she indicated that she was 'cured' and refused any help after that. Truth be told, she stayed sober for two whole weeks but then the turmoil that dwelled in her soul reappeared.

My father hoped that a new incentive in the form of a move abroad would solve the problem, and I honestly thought so too.

We were idiots.

"Please go to sleep," I pleaded in vain.

In response, I heard the tinkling of glass. My mom had probably smacked the wine glass against the wall.

"Why don't you do anything about this?"

Shocked, I turned around.

Mark stood in the same corner as when I first saw him. He was a shadow in the night.

"I'm scared," I replied. At this point I hardly dared to move, let alone get out of bed.

"Your mother doesn't listen to your father and rejects any help. Maybe *you* can convince her." Mark came up to me, sat down at the foot of the bed and looked at me with his green eyes. "This has been going on for way to long."

Yes, for almost a year, if not longer.

"What can I do?"

"Let them know that you've had it. That you will no longer put up with this."

"How?"

Mark glanced at the toybox that stood in the left corner of my room. It was full of toys, Lego, and masks of superheroes like Batman and Spiderman. But there was also a sword sticking out. Its plastic only slightly reflected the moonlight.

"I can't ..." I stammered. "I could never ..."

"If you do nothing, it will only get out of hand!" Mark said.

I looked at him uncertainly.

"I'm going to kill you. You don't deserve to live!"

"Keep your mouth shut and go to sleep!"

I clenched my hands. Mark was right. If I didn't end this, nobody would.

Slowly, I slipped out of bed and staggered to the toybox. I clutched the plastic sword and with Mark at my side, I started to walk through the hallway.

When I arrived at the front door, I stopped. I had a lump in my throat and my heart was pounding so loud that it hurt. I almost lost my grip on the sword.

"Come on," Mark encouraged me. "You can do this. Walk over to them and make them stop!"

"I've told you so many times that you have to listen to me," my mother shouted. *"How often do I have to say it before it gets through your thick head?"*

Another bang followed. A second glass had met its end by hitting the wall.

My feet were pinned to the floor.

"You're afraid, aren't you?" Mark asked.

I nodded.

Mark sighed and walked past me to the corridor. He looked from me to the front door. "Very well," he said eventually. "Then come with me."

I stepped back. "Where to?"

"You don't have the guts to confront your parents, at least not yet. But you hardly ever sleep anymore, do you?"

Again, I nodded.

"Then let me at least distract you for a little while."

"But I can't just ..."

"Then confront your parents."

Frightened, I shook my head.

The decision was made.

We stepped outside. Mark walked in front of me and led the way over winding roads, past old houses and bare plots of land. The moonlight was the only thing that lit up the world around me, which meant that everything else was covered in grim shadows.

Although I only wore my pajamas and walked barefoot, I was not cold. Even the wind had something warm about it.

This wasn't the first time I'd walked this road. I had been here before with my parents. But I couldn't remember that it had looked so … dead before.

The path went up and with every step I took, I heard the roar of the sea getting closer.

We walked as far as we could until we ended up on a bare stone landscape. I looked around me. A thick layer of fog, draped around us like a winter blanket, broke the weak moonlight in a spooky way. I walked a few steps further until my bare feet stood on the edge of a cliff. The wind hit me and pulled at my pajamas. I took a deep breath and inhaled the salty air. A few meters below me, the waves sparkled the bottom rocks. With a wildly roaring sound, the water slammed against them and slid into the cracks and cavities. The sea, which normally displayed shades of blue, green, and indigo, was now enveloped in the shadow of the night.

"Am I dreaming?" I asked Mark.

The boy just smiled and pointed in the direction we just came from. I turned around. My mouth fell open in surprise. The road was gone, just like the rest of the village. What remained were mostly rocks.

There were signs of a forest in the distance. The wind made the branches dance.

"That's where I live!" Mark proudly said.

I looked at him in surprise. "Over there? In the dark? Alone?"

Ashamed, the boy lowered his head. "Well, I don't have anyone else."

My heart ached. "I'm sorry."

Mark looked up. "Don't be. I have you now as a friend, right?" He turned and walked toward the forest.

After a moment of hesitation, I followed him.

The pointed protrusions of the rocks hurt my bare feet, but I ignored the feeling.

I couldn't take my eyes off the forest. There was something out there that I couldn't place. The trees had something ominous and seemed to be watching me. For a moment I even thought I heard a soft chuckle.

"What kind of place is that?" I asked.

"That's where the dark memories are hidden," Mark answered.

"I don't understand."

"It's a place where bad things go."

"And you *live* there?"

Mark just nodded and walked towards the forest.

I stood firmly on the ground. A shiver crept over my body.

"Mark?"

The boy turned and raised his eyebrows questioningly.

"I'm scared."

For a moment, the boy looked at me. "As long as you stay with me, nothing will happen, I promise. Aren't we friends?"

"Will you take me home?" I asked softly.

"Why would you want to go home?" Mark asked. "There is nothing but pain for you there."

"My mother only reacts like that because of the alcohol," I replied. "If she doesn't drink, she's really kind."

There was a brief silence.

"Then you know what to do, don't you?"

I had to think about what Mark meant, but eventually nodded. It was all suddenly very clear.

-6-

The next morning I got up before sunrise.

I slipped out of bed, hurriedly put on my clothes and walked as quietly as I could to the second house. I had never felt so brave before. Although it was quiet and my father and mother were probably both asleep, it was still dark.

I sneaked into the house. My father was sleeping on the couch in the living room, as always when they had a fight. Sometimes he went against her, but most of the time he decided that ignoring her as much as possible was the best solution.

Reluctantly I walked to the kitchen. The door cracked when I opened it. I bit my lip, hoping I didn't wake my dad. I knew I didn't have to worry about my mother. She was in the other house, alone in her bed, passed out from the alcohol.

There were two glasses on the counter. One was still half-filled with white wine, the other had a crack down the side. The bottle next to it was empty.

I opened the fridge and pulled out all the bottles of wine I could find. With the feeling that I was doing something terrible and that I would get into so much trouble for doing this, I poured the contents of the bottles down the sink.

When I was sure that there were no alcoholic substances of any kind left in the entire house, I walked back to the other house. From the corridor, I already saw Mark sitting on my bed. He smiled and clapped his hands inaudibly.

I felt proud.

-7-

Getting rid of the alcohol was of course not the solution. My mother simply bought new bottles.

That evening the shit hit the fan again. A strange voice at the front door woke me up. The neighbors had called the police again. But after a short talk, in which my father promised that my mother would go to sleep and that it would not happen again, it became quiet again. That silence lasted for about thirty minutes. Minutes in which I, clinging to my bed, heard my mother mutter.

When all that pent-up anger inevitably broke out, my body trembled in fear.

"YOU FUCKING BASTARD!"

The scream was followed by a sharp bang and a frightening scream.

I flew out of bed into the hallway and stopped at the open door of my parents' bedroom. On the other side of the room, a glass door opened onto the balcony. I knew that my father had barricaded himself in the living room again. He did that often in an attempt to calm my mother down. If I don't shout back, I'm not that interesting anymore and she will leave me alone, he must have thought.

A dark red substance glistened on the floor of the balcony. Even in the dark I understood what it had to be.

"Mom!" I ran into the room screaming, jerked open the door and stuck my head around the corner.

My mother lay huddled on the balcony. The moonlight lit up her white face. All around her there were glass fragments. One of them was sticking out her left leg. In an attempt to enter the living room, she had kicked in the glass door.

The pool of blood on the balcony grew larger with the second, but I hardly saw it. I stepped through it and hurried to my mother. The warm blood felt syrupy under my bare feet.

My mother saw me approaching and with a stretched hand she reached out to me. Her eyes closed for a second. She opened them again and tried to smile. It was a macabre sight.

The living room door next to me flew open. The glass that was still in the frame clattered on the floor. My father gave me a push. With a smack, I fell on my side in the puddle of blood.

"Damn it, Judith."

"Dad?" I stammered. "Blood ... mom ..." The world revolved around me. I looked at my hands. They were covered in blood, just like my pajamas.

-8-

Not many people attended the funeral. Only me, my father, and his two employees were there.

I think it's impossible for an eight-year-old boy to understand what death really means. And I didn't. Part of me fully realized that it meant that I would never see my mother again. On the other hand, I simply couldn't comprehend it. There was a part of me that expected that somebody would walk up to me to tell me it was all a big joke, that parents only died when they were old and wrinkly. Somehow I still expect that.

My mother had lost so much blood that the medical team that arrived with the ambulance after my father in a panic had called 911 couldn't do anything for her. Before they reached the hospital, she had already died.

That day continued in a haze; an unrealistic nightmare.

My mother's coffin was simple and cheap. My father didn't have the money to buy a fancier one. The wood was uniformly white and the coffin stood beside the freshly dug hole in the ground. There were dozens of memorial stones around it. The ground was hard, more stone and clay than dirt. I felt sorry for my mom that she had to lie in it forever. I wanted so much to stop the funeral. I would do anything to get the power of turning back the time so I could save her. I closed my eyes, hoping that if I could give myself an imaginary friend, I would be able to give me that power too. Needless to say, it didn't work.

I felt a hand on my shoulder. My father hugged me. "I'm sorry, kid," he cried. His tears dripped on my hair. I noticed that my knees nodded uncontrollably. "I should have stopped her."

I wanted to ask him why he didn't, wanted to hit him and push him away, but both my body and mind were paralyzed.

I didn't watch them lower my mother into the ground. I couldn't. Instead, I stared at the dark clouds above me, trying in vain to hold back my tears. This irreversible event had struck a hole in my heart that would always be there. Even now, all these years later, I can still feel it.

-9-

I didn't see Mark that day, nor the days after. That hurt. I thought a true friend was someone who would always be there for you, especially in bad times. But perhaps that was the problem. Mark wasn't real. I had made him up. I felt lonely, and in the weeks that followed, I turned more and more into myself. I barely ate, didn't go to school and lay in my bed all day. I thought about my mother. About the sweet and kind woman she was when she wouldn't drink. Even if I didn't have many memories of her like that. It was like a vicious circle; my sorrow evoked the images in my mind and the images the sorrow.

My teacher apparently heard what had happened. One afternoon she was at our front door, unannounced. She told me and my father that I was very welcome to stay with her for a few days, that a change in environment might distract me from what had happened. But I didn't want that. I now only had one parent, and no matter how angry I was with my father, I also realized that there was no one who cared for him now. He was an adult. He was expected to mourn but then continue with his life. But that wasn't so easy for him, I noticed. And who could blame him for that? He didn't work, walked aimlessly around the house and constantly picked up pictures of him and my mother together. I didn't know a person could weep so much.

Apart from his two employees, he actually had no one who cared about him. Our family members lived in England and although my grandfather and grandmother came by a few days after the funeral, the gap they left behind when they returned back home was bigger than before.

So I took care of him.

I couldn't cook, wash or iron, but I did my best and tried it anyway. It helped me to focus my attention on something else. And although I burned almost all the food I prepared, which meant we had to eat dry bread for the third night in a row, I noticed that my father understood what I was trying to do. And if it slowly got him out of isolation, my goal was achieved.

-10-

It wasn't until many nights later that I saw Mark again.

"Jerry, wake up!"

I slowly opened my eyes. Mark sat next to me,
on the edge of the bed. He looked pale.

I moaned. "Go away!"

"No, you have to come with me!"

I clenched my fist, sat up, and threw him a destructive look. "I don't have to do anything. Go away!"

Uncomprehending, Mark looked at me. "Why do you act like this?" he asked. "I..."

"Where were you, Mark?" I yelled. "I needed you!" "

Mark shook his head. "No, you didn't. You needed to be by yourself, to mourn. I gave you that time. Friends know what the other person really needs."

I sniffed. "You probably didn't even miss me. Go back to your wooden house in the woods. I hope you rot away there."

Mark was visibly shocked by my words. His eyes became watery. The moonlight lit the tear that slid down his cheek. "Of course I missed you, but I did it *for* you."

"Why are you here, Mark?" I snarled.

"The forest behind my house. It ... whispers your name."

"It what?"

"Whispers your name. The trees. Someone or something is waiting for you over there, Jerry. It's calling you."

"Who is calling me?"

Mark glanced away and licked his lips. He muttered something incomprehensible.

"What?" I asked.

"Your mother," my imaginary friend replied. "Or at least I think it's her."

I looked at him in bewilderment and felt anger build up inside me. "Leave me alone, Mark," I said.

"But ..." Mark stammered.

"LEAVE ME ALONE"

Startled, Mark jumped up.

"How dare you?" I shouted. "My mother is dead, Mark! Dead!"

"Well yes, but I really think that ..."

"Go away." This time I begged him. Tears rolled over my cheeks. "Leave me alone!"

"Are you sure you want me to?"

I didn't reply.

"You are just too much of a coward to come with me." For the first time, Mark's voice was contemptuous. "Just like you were too much of a coward to confront your parents." He slowly walked toward the corridor. "But okay, I understand. The wound is still fresh ..." And before I had wiped the tears from my eyes, he was gone.

After that, with Tommy the teddy bear close to me, I sat in my bed crying for a long time. I wanted nothing more than to go to sleep and not only forget Mark's story but also everything else. I wanted to just dream and leave for the land of oblivion. But I couldn't. It continued to gnaw at me, so I finally got out of bed.

I ran outside and across the winding roads that had brought me to Mark's house the last time. He was there. His shadow stood out against the dark blue background and the stars above him. He had waited for me.

"You knew I would come after you," I said.

"Of course!" Mark grinned from ear to ear. "Real friends know each other through and through."

I followed him in silence. When my feet roamed the rocky ground and I heard the roar of the sea again, I turned around. Just like before, the village and the path we had come across had disappeared. They had given way to the forest.

"Do you hear it?" Mark asked.

I nodded. The whispering voice was everywhere, like a lament.

"Jerry ... Jerry ... Jerry ..."

The voice sounded familiar but frightened me at the same time. "Who is it?' I asked softly. I didn't believe it was my mother.

"Do you remember what I told you about what wanders in that forest?"

Hesitantly, I nodded. "Dark memories."

"That's what's left of your mother now," Mark said.

Not fully understanding, I looked at him.

"This is your world, Jerry," Mark clarified. "You must know that by now." He pointed. "That forest is full of your memories."

I was sure I wasn't moving. Yet the forest came closer, as if someone was pulling it in my direction with a string. A wave of dizziness washed through me. I blinked and looked up.

Suddenly, I was in the middle of the forest. With a jerk, I turned around. The rocky ground had disappeared. I didn't even hear the roaring of the waves any longer. Now there were only trees and bushes. The mist swallowed my feet, leaving me unable to see the ground. The canopy of trees largely blocked the moonlight. The rustling of the leaves gave me the shivers, but the whispering voice was the most dominant.

"Jerry ... Jerry ... Jerry ..."

"Mark?" My hands were trembling in fear.

My imaginary friend was no longer with me. Yet I heard his voice, vague and far away.

"You should do this alone, Jerry. Be brave."

At first, I thought he had to stand safely outside the forest, but then I realized that this was not the case. The voice came from deep within me. Mark was me and I was Mark. We were one. It felt good to know he was with me but that didn't take away the fear.

"Jerry ... Jerry ... Jerry ..."

My breathing went faster than ever. I moved slowly. A branch, invisible through the mist, broke under my bare feet. Leaves rustled nearby.

I froze. "Who ...?" I put my hand on my mouth, afraid that someone or something had heard me. The darkness was scary enough by itself. I couldn't bear the thought of someone being with me here.

I knew one thing for sure.

This was a bad place.

I looked around. I saw nothing and heard no more whispers. Everything remained silent.

The silhouette that came from behind a tree had her head bowed. Long black hair hid her face, but I immediately understood that this was my mother.

She walked towards me and stopped in a sliver of moonlight. She was naked. She looked up and smiled at me. It was a warm smile, full of love.

"Jerry," she whispered. She held out her hand to me. And my soul broke. All the sorrow that I had been burying in the deep part of my brain for the last couple of days, came out. My legs were shaking and I collapsed. The wind held me in its arms and I rocked back and forth on my knees.

I cried.

"Mom?"

My mother approached me. She kneeled before me. "You have to help me, Jerry."

I shrugged my nose and looked at her uncomprehendingly.

"I'm so sorry." Her voice sang in the night.

Somehow I realized that I was dreaming. My mother was dead, I shouldn't be able to see her. But it was a thought that I suppressed. What did it matter that this wasn't real? It didn't make this any less real. My mother sat in front of me, sober for the first time in a long time, and I loved her.

But I suddenly realized that that wasn't true. Or at least, there was another feeling that prevailed: anger.

"I'm so lonely down here," my mother said. I could read the grief in her eyes. "It's so cold and I can't leave here."

"What do you mean?" I asked.

"I'm trapped here, caught in your mind."

I felt a tear slide down my cheek. "But isn't that the only place where you can live?"

My mother shook her head.

Mark spoke in my mind. "She belongs in your heart, Jerry."

I didn't get it. Then why was she here?

"Because you didn't forgive her. Because you hate what she did to you and that she wasn't strong enough to stay away from the alcohol, even though she knew it was bad for her and her family."

"That's not true!" I cut him off. But, of course, that was a lie.

"Help me," my mother begged again.

I suddenly realized that I couldn't do that, no matter how much I wanted it. The fact was that I *did* blame her. Forgiveness is not always easy. You must feel it with all your heart. I didn't.

I stood up. My mother remained seated on the ground. She looked at me pleadingly.

"Please, get me out of here."

"I'm sorry," I whispered. And with those words, I ran away from her as fast as I could.

Bathed in sweat, I woke up screaming. My pajamas stuck to my skin. The smell of my sweat was nauseous.

I knew it hadn't been real, just a dream, but I also knew that my mother lived on in that same dream, which made it more real again.

The bedroom door opened with a jerk. A shadow appeared in the opening. A hand slid towards the switch and the bright light blinded me.

I hastily put a hand over my eyes.

"Jerry, what's wrong?" My father asked.

He came and sat next to me on the bed. A hand went through my wet hair. "Did you have a bad dream?"

I nodded. My eyes adjusted to the light. I lowered my hand and looked at my father. Because of the bags under his eyes and his pale skin color, he looked even worse than the last few days. That hurt me. I was hoping that he would slowly begin to process my mother's death.

I glanced sideways at my clock radio. The red figures indicated that it was three o'clock in the morning.

"Were you dreaming about Mom?"

I looked at him with wide eyes. I wanted to ask him how he knew that, but it occurred to me that it was logical for him to think so. I nodded.

My father gently squeezed my hand. "Come with me." He stood up and walked down the hall.

I slipped out of bed and followed him thoughtfully.

The king sized bed in my father's bedroom was littered with scrapbooks and individual photos. He picked up the wedding album. "She was so beautiful that day."

I swallowed and sat down beside him. We leafed through the album in silence.

"I know I shouldn't do this right now," my father said after a while. His voice cracked. "That it doesn't help to process it. But I don't want to forget her, Jerry."

Now it was my turn to squeeze his hand.

"I knew she was a different person when she

drank," my father continued. "And we should have sought help years ago. But she didn't want to. The woman she really was, without alcohol ... God, I miss her. "

"I don't remember her without alcohol," I said. Embarrassed, I turned my head away from him.

"Of course you do. But you are giving the wrong memories priority." In the photo he took, I was about four years old. I sat on my mother's back and we walked through an amusement park. We laughed. My father showed me a few more pictures; lost memories of a wonderful time. I slowly began to remember how safe I had always felt in her arms.

"That's how she must live on in your memory, Jerry. Not the woman the alcohol made her become."

"Why did she have to drink, Dad?" My voice broke. I wanted to keep myself strong for him, but failed hopelessly. Tears rolled down my cheeks.

"Stress," he answered. "We both had such big dreams for this place, for the diving school, for you. Unfortunately, not all dreams come true. She could escape in alcohol. It allowed her to continue to dream and to hide reality." He grabbed my chin and forced me to look at him. "But she loved us, you know that right?"

I slowly nodded. "Why did she keep drinking?"

"Alcohol can be dangerous, Jerry. She was not strong enough to get rid of the chains that an addiction like that brings. She might have been dangerous when she had alcohol, but deep down, she was the victim. She just didn't see it ... didn't want to see it ..." He swallowed. "And neither did I, at least not in time."

My gaze wandered over the bed. The photos made me relive the past for a couple of seconds. I was five again and walked hand in hand with my mother on the beach. I was six years old, my mother surprised me with a guitar on my birthday. I was seven and sat on an airplane with my parents on my way to Portugal. There were only smiles.

I noticed that the anger towards my mother slowly faded. Instead, another emotion emerged: pity.

The fact was that I did love my mother. I always had. She had made mistakes. Terrible mistakes, but still.

"Everyone makes mistakes, Jerry. That's what makes us human."

It was my mother's voice. It made me look around. I realized almost immediately that it had sounded in my head. After all, she was trapped in there, in the forest where my bad memories were hidden.

Mark appeared in the doorway. He smiled.

I smiled back.

-12-

The world faded away even before I was back in bed. Reality dissolved like wrinkles in water. I had left my nightlight on, but now the light was swallowed up until the darkness was complete. Waves lashed right next to me. The wind howled. Slowly, the forms returned. Eventually, I was able to see the stones and trees.

I sat on the floor in front of the forest. Mark was standing next to me and smiled pointing at the trees. I nodded and stood up. My heart was beating in my throat. Still, I was calm. I knew why I was here.

The bushes rustled as I entered the forest. Although the canopy above me was incredibly dense, the moon illuminated me with every step I took on the narrow road, as is only possible in dreams.

"You came back."

One moment I was alone, the next my mother stood in front of me. She looked at me lovingly.

I nodded. "This is a bad place. You don't belong here."

My mother smiled and gave me her hand. I put my hand in hers. Her touch felt warm, familiar. Confidently, I escorted her out of the forest.

Side by side we walked past dozens of trees and bushes. I hardly saw where I was walking. My eyes were completely focused on my mother.

"I love you, Jerry," she whispered.

At that moment, the last bit of resentment melted in my soul. "I love you too."

Mark was waiting for us, grinning, nodding approvingly.

Suddenly, my mother's hand disappeared from mine.

With a jerk, I turned around. "Mom?" I shouted in panic.

She was gone. In the place where she just stood, only a few bushes and branches danced back and forth in the wind.

"Don't panic, Jerry," Mark responded calmly. "You have forgiven her. She is no longer there."

"Then where is she?" I stammered, afraid I had made a big mistake.

Mark said nothing. It wasn't necessary. I already knew the answer.

My hand slid to my chest. The place where my heart was felt warm and I realized that I would forever carry her with me.

-13-

Just like the forest, I never saw Mark again after that night, but I didn't mind. Imaginary friends only appear when you really need them, I suppose. And that was no longer the case.

In the weeks that followed, my father took over the role of adult again and he also decided to return to England. Sometimes not all dreams can be realized, and it is important to see reality. I would learn that lesson years later when I was an adult. I made some friends at my new school. I think the events in Portugal gave me more confidence.

I still regularly think about my mother. It feels good to know that she is always with me and watches over me. Sometimes I think I hear her voice when I'm at a crossroads in my life and have to make a decision. That she is there to guide me in a way only mothers can.

- The End -

Can you help?

Thank You For Reading My Book!

Please allow me to personally thank you and give you a gift. <u>Click here to watch the video.</u>

I really appreciate all of your feedback, and I love hearing what you have to say.

Reviews are very important for an author. When I get more reviews on my books it allows them to stay more visible, so I can spend more time writing rather than marketing. So if you want me to put books out more quickly, please leave a review on this one!

The review doesn't have to be long. Just a few words and some stars is enough to help me out.

Thank you so much!

J. Sharpe

Other books by J. Sharpe

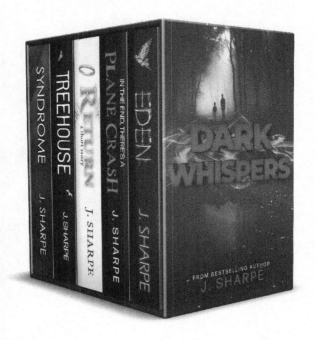

Five books, access to a bonus story, and
hundreds of pages of suspense, horror, and
magic realism fill this box set by award
nominee and bestselling author J. Sharpe.
Grab them all for one low price now!

Click here to download

EDEN

*WILL YOU SURVIVE
A NEW PLAGUE?*

J. SHARPE

Nobody will survive a new plague?

Angels: they're among us. I would know. There's one trapped inside of me. But the image you probably have of these "helpers of God" is wrong, I guarantee it. They are all maniacal assholes.

Anna Meisner awakes, naked and afraid, tied to a chair in a dark room. Across from her sits a woman who is her spitting image. With tears in her eyes, the woman puts a gun against her head and kills herself. Anna is not found until days later and in a state of hypothermia, moments from dying. But when she wakes in the hospital, she finds that the police don't see her as a victim, but as a suspect. It's the beginning of a series of catastrophic events in which she has no choice but to play a part. Is this the end of humanity?

Eden (nominated for a Bastaard Fantasy Award) is a post-apocalyptic suspense novel. If you like fast-paced books with a lot of twists and like to search for all the hidden references of the bible, then you will definitely love this book.

Download the first few chapters for free by clicking here

To pick up a copy on Amazon click here

HOW DO YOU FIND SOMEONE WHO EVERYONE CLAIMS DOESN'T EXIST?

"A REAL PAGETURNER"

SYNDROME

—— J. SHARPE ——

SUSPENSE

How do you find someone who everyone claims doesn't exist?

It starts as a game but ends in terror. Soon it becomes clear. Someone is chasing them.

After an accident, Peter's mother is in a coma and his father is unable to cope. Because of this, Peter has no other choice than to drop out of school, start a job and take over the care of his little sister. One day he picks her up from school to take her to the mall. Then the unthinkable happens. They're being followed. And their pursuer is not from this world...

When his sister disappears, Peter starts to notice that more things are terribly wrong. Especially when no one seems to remember her. Even his father claims he never had a daughter. It's almost as if she never existed...

Will he be able to save his sister? Or is she lost forever?

Syndrome is a suspense novel that keeps you on the edge of your seat. If you like fast-paced stories, with plot twists that keep you surprised with every turn of the page, then you will definitely love this book by award nominee and bestselling author J.Sharpe.

Syndrome was nominated for a Harland Award and A Bastaard Award.

Pick up Syndrome today, if you dare!

Read the first chapters for free by <u>clicking here</u>

<u>Download the complete book here.</u>

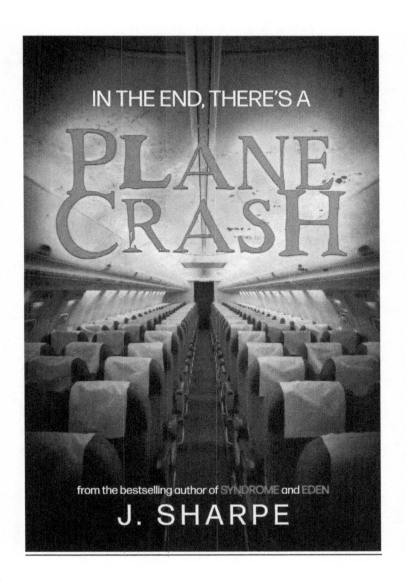

IN THE END, THERE'S A

PLANE CRASH

from the bestselling author of SYNDROME and EDEN

J. SHARPE

At 16000 feet, horror strikes flight 447

During a flight from Amsterdam to Madrid, an airplane crashes on a solid cloud. Then more than half of the passengers disappear...

Eighteen-year-old Linda is on her first flight as a stewardess. So far, she hates everything about it. The constant humming of the engines, the nagging of the passengers, the crying babies... Luckily the plane is almost at its destination. Little does she know her body will touch the ground in a way she had never expected before.

Trapped more than a thousand feet high on a cloud, she and everyone onboard find out the hard way that there had gone something terribly wrong. And not just with the airplane.

In the end, there's a plane crash is a suspense/horror story. If you like pageturners with a lot of twists and blood-curdling horror, then you will definitely love this book by award nominee and bestselling author J.Sharpe.

Pick up *In the end, there's a plane crash* today and enjoy the flight!

Click here to download a copy.

Wait, there's more?

Don't forget to grab your copy of *In the arms of my love* and *Treehouse* for free.

To get access to this one and other free books simply <u>click here</u> or go to my website: www.jsharpefiction.com

You can also follow me on social media.

Facebook: J.Sharpe
Instagram: jsharpebooks

About the author

J. Sharpe – a pseudonym for Joris van Leeuwen (1986) – has written several mystery thrillers, fantasy novels, and short stories. His work is often compared with novels by authors such as Stephen King, Dean Koontz, and Peter Straub. He was shortlisted for the prestigious Dutch sci-fi and fantasy Harland Award in 2016 and 2018, for the best fantasy book written in that year. He is known for not sticking to one genre only. His thrillers, for example, usually contain elements of horror, sci-fi, or fantasy, and vice versa.

Made in the USA
Coppell, TX
07 February 2023

12400427R00042